Ghosts of Ohio's Lincoln Highway

© Bruce Carlson 2010

All rights reserved. No part of this book may be reproduced or transmitted in any form or by any means, electronic or mechanical, including photocopying, recording or by any informational storage or retrieval system, except by a reviewer who may quote brief passages in a review to be printed in a magazine or newspaper without permission in writing from the publisher.

Table of Contents

Finally Home 13

The Unfortunate Child 23

Racing In The Treetops 33

Keepin' 'Em Up 45

One More Game 53

The South End Two-Step 61

25% Off 71

The Handyman 81

The Worn Spot 89

The Return Of The Ring 97

Pickled Liver 103

The Inconvenience 109

The reader should understand that we were able to obtain some of these stories only if we promised to obscure some of the actual identity of persons and/or property. This required us to occasionally use fictitious names. In such cases, the names of the people and/or the places are not to be confused with actual places or actual persons living or dead.

This book is dedicated to all the folks along our beautiful Lincoln Highway here in Ohio who shared stories with us.

Finally Home

For almost all of his life, Russ Morgan had lived in the Midwest, a long way from the Tennessee River.

Back in the 1920s when Russ was growing up out in Van Wert, he lived with distant relatives. That home of the Jackson family was the only one he had known because he came to be raised by the Jacksons shortly after the death of his parents. Both his father, Russell L. Morgan, and his mother, Ruth P. Morgan, were killed in a car wreck when Russ was less than a year old.

The sum total of what Russ knew about his parents was that they were killed in a wreck back east somewhere and their last name was Morgan.

This account was put together in 1986 by Russ' "sister," Joan Jackson, who did a lot of investigation of Russ' background after Russ died in 1984.

Joan was aware that there were others in the relationship who had information about Russ' background. It was from them that she pulled together all the facts that constitute this account of the life of Russ.

So, while Joan would eventually learn a lot about her "brother," she was unaware of all that while she and Russ were growing up out in Van Wert.

Russ' childhood was that of any midwestern child. He and Joan had been well cared for by the Jacksons, and Russ felt like he was a Jackson, just as was Joan, his "sister."

The Jacksons had not adopted Russ, so he kept his birth name, Russ Morgan.

There was, like in all families, a situation that was unique to that particular family. In this family the unique thing was a mystery. It was a mystery about a strange gift that Russ would get each birthday, each May Day and each Christmas.

That gift first showed up on May Basket Day in 1923, the first of May. That was the first May Day that Russ was with the Jacksons.

While May 1 is no longer an occasion for gift giving among children, it was an important day in the life of kids back then.

Each May 1, the kids would deliver ornate little baskets, each filled with candy, to other kids. The custom was for the gift-giving child to knock on the door of his friend's place, set the basket by the door, and then run off before the object of his affection would discover who had left the basket.

There was an element of childhood romance about the giving of May Baskets much as there is yet today with Valentine's Day.

The giving and receiving of May Baskets was a nice little custom that was a source of a lot of fun for the children back then.

And, it was on May 1, 1923, when a number of May Day Baskets showed up on the porch at the Jackson home. Joan and Russ both prepared a number of May Baskets for their friends, and each received a number of those gaily-decorated little symbols of affection.

All of those baskets were decorated and contained a few pieces of candy, that is, all but one exception. That one exception contained a few ounces of dirt and a note. The note simply read:

"Come Home"

Now, dirt in a May Basket was unheard of. In fact, a note in a May Basket was rare. But, that dirt was really a mystery. Why would anyone put dirt in a May Basket?

The kids couldn't understand it, and neither could Mr. and Mrs. Jackson.

The basket was a very nice one, nicely decorated and in good taste. But the dirt: Why that dirt? And who left it?

There simply weren't any answers to those questions.

And, to further confound the issue, the dirt was red. Now, anyone with any sense at all there in the Midwest knew that dirt was anywhere from dark brown to black. Red dirt was

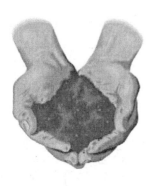

simply out of the question. Folks knew that out west farther, there were places where the dirt would tend to yellow, but that there was a rare exception. Dirt was dirt colored; that is brown to black, and red dirt was like a green sky or a blue lawn. That sort of thing simply didn't happen.

But, there it was in that May Basket. At Russ' age, all he knew was that………..for some reason, there wasn't any candy in that one particular May Basket, that being all a two-year-old would care, of course.

The mystery deepened considerably on August 11, on Russ' birthday, when a gift showed up again on the Jackson's front porch.

There was no hint on that package of who left the gift…………..only the note:

"COME HOME"

Again, the content was a mystery. It was only a few ounces of that strange red dirt.

This odd event happening twice was cause for some concern there at the Jackson home, but was finally dismissed as somebody's childish prank.

The whole issue slipped from Russ' mind in a matter of minutes, and shortly his "mom" and "dad" put that behind them, also.

That is, they did until Christmas when it happened the third time. Same contents and same note.

This was starting to irritate Mr. And Mrs. Jackson, but it, too, was soon forgotten in the busy holiday season.

The following year was a repeat of what had happened in 1923. And, again, in '25 and '26.

Each occasion reopened the issue of who was doing that...........and why. And what was with that strange colored soil.

The years that followed brought that odd gift of nicely wrapped red dirt each May 1, each August 11 and each December 25.

And, each time the family would wonder, but couldn't come up with an answer. The childish prank idea didn't make sense after years of this happening. But no one could come up with a better answer.

And the situation continued on into Russ' adulthood.

Russ left home, married and started his own family. Those odd gifts continued, three times a year. By the 1980s, the practice of observing May Day was over with. This is, except at the home of Russ and his wife, Darlene.

Darlene was amazed at that gift three times a year, and found it difficult to believe it had been going on all those years.

Darlene talked to Joan, her sister-in-law, who confirmed Russ' story. That present showed up three times a year, just like clockwork, and over fifty years hadn't seen a change in the routine..........same gift, same message.

"COME HOME"

1984 found the couple living near the Tennessee River, a long way from Van Wert, Ohio.

That was the year Russ died. It was a heart condition that caused his death in March 1984.

The issue of a burial site came up, of course. Darlene and Joan talked about that. The elder Jacksons had been buried in separate cemeteries, he in that of his hometown and she was buried near her family a couple hundred miles away.

Darlene and Joan came to the conclusion that since there was no one place where the Jacksons were buried, there was no point in having the body sent anywhere, but it would be just fine to bury Russ there in a little country cemetery on the banks of the Tennessee.

And so the interment was there in Tennessee.

Both Joan, as Russ' "sister," and Darlene, his wife, were there at the funeral, as well as other relatives.

The service at the church was over and the funeral party gathered at the local cemetery.

As is traditional, the family all sat together in folding chairs in the front row, just a couple of feet from the casket.

A portion of the excavated dirt was exposed there, showing out from under a fake grass blanket.

Joan elbowed Darlene to get her attention. Darlene looked at her sister-in-law to see what she wanted.

She saw a shocked and wide-eyed Joan motioning for Darlene to see what she was looking at, that dirt showing out from under that fake green turf-like material.

As soon as Darlene saw that dirt, she realized, as had Joan, that the dirt showing there was the same red dirt that showed up in those gifts that came three times a year.

Those were two thoroughly shocked ladies sitting there, each with their thoughts in turmoil as they tried to piece together the color of that dirt and those messages through the years, each one saying:

"COME HOME"

Joan and Darlene could hardly wait to get outside the funeral tent to talk about this odd twist of events. Here, their Russ was being buried in that strange red dirt.

As soon as the people were dismissed, they stepped outside the tent to discuss this.

Suddenly, it was Darlene's turn to elbow her sister-in-law.

Joan's eyes followed those of Darlene, who was looking at the two graves next to Russ'. They had paid no attention to the neighboring graves up until now since they had no reason to know or care who would lie buried next to Russ.

But, now they saw. The two graves were………..Russell L. Morgan and Ruth P. Morgan.

It was then that the decades-old mystery of those gifts became clear. It was then that Joan and Darlene knew where those gifts had been coming from………..and that Russ had, indeed, come home.

The Unfortunate Child

I'm going to include this story in this book in spite of the fact that the fellow who told it to me also told me that he was going to lie to me about the dates and the names of the people involved.

He explained that if all the facts came out, there'd be a bunch of his relatives in lots of trouble.

He told me he'd be truthful about all the other details, including where all this happened.

With that, this guy proceeded to tell me about his sister's experience here in Upper Sandusky just three or four years ago. He shared with me the fact that his sister was from Upper Sandusky just as he was, but she and her husband had moved to California.

While in California, she got pregnant and put herself under the care of their family doctor out there.

At some point along the process, she had an ultrasound and discovered she was going to have twins. That ultrasound clearly showed two little heads, so this gal (we'll call her Mary) got all excited about having twins.

Twins were not common in the family so she decided that was pretty cool.

She had asked the fellow who told the story not to share that twins information with anyone else until subsequent ultrasounds could confirm the whole thing.

And, she did have another ultrasound. That one was the one that brought her world crashing down around her. Her pregnancy suddenly went from the most wonderful thing that had ever happened to her…………..to being a tragic situation.

During the course of that second ultrasound that was being administered by a nurse, the nurse suddenly became very uncommunicative about the whole thing.

Mary had the distinct impression that something was seriously wrong.

As she was contemplating that, the nurse announced that she would get the doctor in there.

Mary became even more apprehensive then, fearing that anything that would necessitate the doctor's presence might well be something really serious.

Her speculation proved correct. The doctor did a lot of studying of that ultrasound before he told Mary that they had a problem.

"A problem?"

"Yes, Mary, I have some pretty awful news to share with you."

Mary was too fearful to even ask for the details, but the doctor went on.

"Mary, you'll recall we saw the two heads quite distinctly the last time we did an ultrasound, but had difficulty picking up on the bodies.

"Well, this time we should have no problem with that at all. In fact, we should be able to pick up on their genders quite easily today.

"The problem is extremely rare. In fact, it's one I've never encountered before. It is rare enough to approach being impossible.

"But, it is possible and, unfortunately, you are a victim of it."

"What in the world are you talking about, Doctor?"

"Mary, the two heads are very visible, and the one single body is very clear."

"The one single body?"

"Yes, Mary, I'm sorry, but that's the situation."

"Doctor, are you telling me I am carrying a child with two heads?"

Even as Mary said those words, she felt overcome with nausea, nausea spawned by shock and fear.

"I'm sorry, Mary, but that's the situation."

Mary knew after that the doctor was talking, but heard nothing. Her mind was racing along, almost out of control.

Mary and her totally shocked husband talked well into the night after that ultrasound.

It was well after midnight by the time they made their decision as to what they would do.

The next day, Mary made a point of chatting with a number of her friends, sharing with them the exciting news that the couple would be moving back to Upper Sandusky. She told them that Tom (not his real name) had gotten a really nice job offer back in Upper Sandusky and that they'd be moving within days.

And, they did.

The fellow telling this story explained, at that point, how he and his wife got involved in his sister's problem.

Mary enlisted her sister-in-law's aid, this guy's wife, to help her in her plan.

The sister-in-law had had some training in midwifery. Mary felt that the sister-in-law, Jane (again, not a real name) could deliver that monster for her.

Mary and Tom moved in with Jane and her husband in the middle of the night. There were no suitcases, no moving van, no other evidence of their even being there.

Tom found a job way off in Kenton where they felt no one would ever learn he was living in Upper Sandusky, and Mary never left the house where she could be seen.

So things went until Mary had her child with the assistance of Jane.

The only people aware of what was happening were the four of them. Mary had told her doctor in California that she would put herself under the care of a doctor where she was moving.

That California doctor offered to share medical records with the doctor, but went nowhere. Mary got what medical records she could and said she'd give them to the new doctor.

The fellow telling this story said that the baby was "disposed of." He wouldn't elaborate on that whatsoever, of course.

All this seemed to be a lot of discussion with no evidence of a ghost. It was also a tale that certainly explained the man's reluctance to identify himself or to provide any information one could use to trace those people.

It was obvious that a crime had been committed, no doubt the crime of murder.

At this point, the writer of this story began to get uncomfortable with the very limited information he had about the situation.

"But, what about a ghost story?" I asked.

"Well, this is a ghost story. Lemme explain."

With that, the fellow went on to explain how his sister and brother-in-law went public and suddenly "showed up" here in Upper Sandusky.

The pair got jobs here, bought a house and set up housekeeping.

Jane and her husband welcomed the "newcomers," and all appeared cool.

Time went by with Mary ending up pregnant again.

That pregnancy resulted in her delivering a fine young boy.

That child had a nursery in a room near the bedroom of Mary and Tom, and everything went well until the boy was about two months old.

Like any child, this one would cry at night. It didn't take long for Mary to learn one particular sound of her child crying. Like any other baby, the child's voice was unique to himself, even at that early age.

It was late one night when Mary awoke to the sound of a crying child.

She thought, at the time, that the child didn't sound quite normal, but figured that maybe he had a touch of a cold or something.

Even as she was scurrying down the hall, she was thinking about what she'd have to do about the baby getting a cold. If it wasn't one dang thing with a new baby, it was another.

All of a sudden, just as Mary was going through the doorway into the nursery, she had the distinct impression she heard another baby crying, not one instead of hers, but one in addition to hers.

That, of course, was impossible. Extra babies don't just show up that way.

By now she was in the room, heading for the crib to comfort the child.

It was at that point that the volume of the crying sound went up as well as the apparent number of voices represented by all that noise.

Shaking the sleep from her head, Mary tried to figure out what was going on. Having gotten fully awake, Mary made a remarkable discovery.

She discovered that her baby there right at her fingertips was crying all right, but the sounds of two other crying babies were coming to her from somewhere over by the dresser.

There was no way in the world for this to be happening, but there were those two voices over there by that dresser.

After just a little patting of the baby put it back to sleep, those sounds from over by the dresser persisted.

Totally mystified as to how this could be, Mary flipped the light on.

That simple act was a turning point in her life.

Over by the dresser, just two or three feet off the floor, was a child, as if supported in the air………a child with no clothes on.

As if it wasn't shocking enough to see a baby there, it was even more shocking for Mary to see that it was far from a normal child. It was one with one body and two heads.

Each of those heads was crying, each with its own distinctive sound.

All the crying and Mary's sudden scream got Tom out of his bed to see what was going on.

Tom's world was never the same after he dashed into the nursery……………that uncharacteristically well-lit nursery.

He found the baby asleep, his wife lying in a crumpled heap on the floor and a sight over by the dresser he simply couldn't fathom. There was that same vision that had greeted his wife.

Later, after Mary had recovered, the two of them compared notes and agreed as to what they had seen.

While the images evaporated shortly after Tom had come into the room, the recollection of that sight remained with both Mary and Tom to this day.

While neither Mary nor Tom had been believers in the existence of ghosts, that sure changed their minds that evening.

And there were recurrences of that situation. Similar appearances came to one or both of the pair thereafter, the latest one happening a few weeks prior to this writing.

While we don't know many of the circumstances that led to the disposal of that baby, it certainly appears that foul play was involved, and that this hapless couple has been harassed by the ghost of that unfortunate child.

Racing In The Treetops

When we look at a row of trees up against the blue sky, we can see there is a definite line of departure as the green from the trees changes to the blue of the sky. That line up there is well defined, seemingly sufficiently well defined that one could skip along up there on that green as if one were skipping along on the green surface that separates the green of some sod from the blue of the sky.

We also know that while that line can be well defined, it sure isn't a surface upon which we could walk. There is no substance to that seemingly definite surface. All it is is the ends of some flimsy end twigs and sprigs of the trees. We know that were we to find ourselves up there, that we would come crashing down through the trees, perhaps a one-way trip to the line that separates the quick from the dead.

The only things up there flitting around that unsubstantial surface are birds and bugs that aren't in the practice of falling anywhere.

We are so accustomed to recognizing the unsubstantial nature of that surface up there, we don't even think about it being a surface.

So, when the Jacob boys from Wooster were out squirrel hunting along a creek that emptied into the Killbuak River, and watching up in the trees for their dinner, they got the surprise of their young lives. They both saw the two horses with riders riding bareback at the same time. Way up where the green of the very tops of the trees changed to the blue of the sky was a horse race going on at full gallop.

All thoughts of squirrel hunting came to an end as those two realized what they were seeing. Somehow, up there in the air, was a horse race going on! They could hear nothing, no clammer of hooves, no heavy breathing of horses at full gallop, or any of the shouts and whooping and hollering that usually accompanies a good spirited race………just the sight of two fellows at full gallop up in an area where there should have been only bugs and birds.

It was a bay and a pinto, the bay being ever-so-slightly ahead, and apparently pulling away from the pinto.

The boys averted their eyes only momentarily as they looked at each other, hoping to find, in the eyes of the other, some explanation for what they were seeing.

The bay and the pinto were still in sight, rounding the crown of a sycamore tree, when three more showed up behind them. They were two sorrels and a dun.

Again the boys could see the horses and see the riders, but could hear nothing from that small knot of horses and riders.

What they were seeing was so impossible that they were left speechless with awe and wonder.

Then, as quickly as all those horses and their riders had appeared, they were gone.

It took a minute for the fellows to even figure out what questions they had for each other. It wasn't an "iffy" or "maybe" sort of thing. Those horses were there, and the riders were there. The boys compared notes as to what all that looked like. They were in agreement regarding the number and color of the horses. They were in agreement about the appearance of the riders. They appeared to be well-bronzed farm boys, kind of old-fashioned looking, but definitely farm boys.

The brothers agreed that only one of the five had a saddle, that being the dun-colored horse. They even had both noticed that all five of the horses neck-reined except the pinto. That one stood out due to the awkward handling of the animal since it didn't neck-rein.

The boys lost all interest in continuing to hunt squirrels. The experience they had so overwhelmed them, that was all they could think of.

There was no way in the world for there to have been horses and riders out there, but there was.

At first, the boys decided they would tell no one about what they had seen. They knew that anyone with any sense would refused to believe them. Neither one of them wanted to be in a position of defending the indefensible, so agreed they'd breathe not a word about what they saw.

But, as the pair walked back to the house there on the edge of Wooster, they could sure talk about it between themselves. They didn't have to convince each other about what they had seen. They both saw it and they saw the same thing.

The closer they got to the house, the more they found themselves in total awe over what they had seen, and their resolve to keep it a secret started to erode.

By the time they got to the house, they had completely changed their minds and couldn't wait to tell everybody about their experience out in the woods that day.

The two boys were Arnie Jacobs and Ted Jacobs. The two of them agreed that Arnie would tell the folks about the whole thing and Ted would be there to back him up.

"The folks" there at the house were their two parents, a kid sister and their grandfather who lived with them.

So, they held to their plan. Arnie told the story and Ted was there eager to back up his brother's tale. They knew this was going to be a hard story to believe, and they wanted folks to know they were dead serious about this.

The two boys gathered everybody there in the kitchen so they'd all hear about what had happened out in the woods and proceeded with their report of their experience.

It didn't take but a few sentences before it was apparent to the two that they weren't going to be believed.

They had no sooner got to the point in their story when the second group of horses and riders showed up, the two sorrels and the dun made their appearances and the boys' mother wanted to smell their breaths.

The two of them found this pretty aggravating. Not only did their mother not believe them, but assumed they had been drinking.

Their kid sister had already started to mess with her doll she had carried in the kitchen with her. Apparently the story was so obviously a made-up one that she had lost interest.

The boys' looks at their father let them know right away that their dad was sitting there trying to figure out what the two were up to, and what cockamamie thing they had going that would lead them to come up with such a tale. They could tell he was trying to figure out what they were hiding and why.

Grandpa just sat there with a sort of funny look on his face like he always had.

It was then the two looked at each other, each realizing that they had made a mistake in telling about what they had seen. Obviously, they were not going to be believed.

Ted was at the point where he was about to storm out of the house, irritated over how people weren't going to believe a perfectly sound fact. The two of them had seen those horses up there, and that was all there was to it!

Arnie was getting angry also. Both boys realized they had made a mistake and were angry both at themselves for telling their story and their family for not believing it.

Ted had slammed down his coat and was already turning to the door when the boys' grandfather spoke up.

"Hold on there, boys. Don't go stompin' off. That ain't gonna accomplish nothin', and 'sides, I got a question for you."

Neither of the two of them was in the mood for any questions. Further talk seemed like rubbing salt in their wounds, and they didn't want to discuss it.

"Now, tell me fellows. I want you to tell me if you noticed anything about how any of those horses reined. Did any of 'em not neck-rein?"

That question caught both of the boys by surprise. Not only was the question asked sincerely as if the old fellow really wanted an answer, but the question was odd in that it addressed an issue that both of them had noticed. They had both picked up on the failure of that pinto to neck-rein, and here their grandfather was asking about that very thing.

It took Arnie a moment to switch from anger to civilly answer a perfectly civil question.

"Er............well, as a matter of fact............yeah, there was one that didn't. You don't often see a saddle horse that doesn't neck-rein, but one of 'em didn't. It was the..............."

At this point the old man interrupted his grandson.

"No, don't tell me which one didn't neck-rein. I'll tell you which one it was. It was the pinto, wasn't it?"

It took a moment for all that to register on Arnie. He was not a bit ready for such a thing from his grandfather. Not only was the old man being nonjudgmental on this whole thing, but told him accurately which one it was that didn't neck-rein.

"Yeah, but………..but how………."

The grandfather interrupted again, asking about the bridles used on the various horses. The boys had to think about a couple of the things the old man asked, but came up with answers they agreed upon.

This conversation with their grandfather was rapidly becoming the second awesome thing the boys had experienced that day.

Here the old man was asking questions that suggested that he had knowledge of what the boys had seen.

Eagerly, the two of them fell to asking questions of their grandfather, trying to figure out how he fit into this whole thing.

The old man asked his daughter and her husband to sit back down, he wanted to tell about a situation that undoubtedly bore on this whole thing.

The two adults did as requested. They had listened to the dialogue between the old fellow and their two sons, and realized that something really, really odd might be afoot here.

The boys' kid sister laid down her doll, wondering what was going on.

With that, the old man told about a situation back when he was a child. He told of how that area where his grandsons had been that day had been a relatively open area back when he was a child, and how the bigger boys used to have horse races there, down along that creek.

The old man told of how he was far too young to participate in those races, but he lived in a cabin near that area and would take every opportunity to go over there when the big kids would gather for their races.

He told of how he was so enthralled with what the big boys got to do that he did a pretty good job of knowing who rode what, and something about each of the boys and each of the horses.

He recalled that dun his grandsons spoke of, and he recalled how the Stephens kid rode a horse, a pinto horse, that did not neck-rein. Failure to neck-rein was such a unique problem for a saddle horse that it stuck out in his memory.

As the old man told about the various neighbor kids, their mounts and the makeshift equipment that farm boys tended to use in their riding, more came back to him. By the time he got over with his tale, he had recalled who had owned the bay and the two sorrels. He recalled the shoddy bridle one of the sorrels wore, and the other had a bridle with overly long reins.

The Warren kid from down the road had that sorrel equipped with the long, long reins and he recalled how the animal had tripped over its reins one time.

The Jacob boys sat there in open-mouthed amazement, hearing all that.

By this time they had sat down, no longer ready to stomp out of the house in anger.

And, by this time, the boys' parents came to realize that the boys hadn't been drinking and had, indeed, seen something that day that had some foundation in reality.

Suddenly there were four people attempting to pepper the old fellow with questions, but he didn't answer any of them. He continued on with his story.

He told of how the neighbor boys had gathered for a race, and had temporarily taken refuge under a large tree since it had started to rain and storm a bit.

"I was off, sittin' under another tree since my ma wouldn't let me get too close to those big boys with their horses. She was afraid I'd get stomped on, I guess. Anyways, I was settin' under that tree watching the fellows, hoping the rain would hold off so they could get on with their race."

It was apparent that Grandpa was slipping back into memories of his childhood, memories he hadn't visited for a long, long time. He spoke as if all this had happened just yesterday instead of all those years ago.

"I was watchin' those fellows and all of a sudden there was the biggest bang and that big old tree the guys was settin' under was all covered up with smoke.

"I wasn't big enough at the time to realize what had happened, but folks figured it all out pretty quick. Lightning had hit that tree and traveled down the trunk and hit those fellows and their horses. All those guys must have been touchin' each other or awfully close since there was a bunch of them all crowded under one tree.

"That lightning did its thing, and it killed all of the horses and all but one of the boys. The one who didn't get killed never was right after that. Folks figured it fried his brain, and he never did get over it."

The kitchen was suddenly very quiet, the only sound being the teakettle on the stove that had heated up and was whistling its message that the water inside was boiling.

Mrs. Jacobs moved the teapot off the burner and each was left with their thoughts.

It was apparent that there not only was something to what the boys had seen, but there was a lot to it.

Grandpa was eighty-four at the time and was telling about an incident when he was a child, so it had to have happened over seventy years earlier.

Apparently some young bucks who had been in the practice of racing their horses down in a pasture never did quite get over it. A bunch of boys who died together apparently came back for another race down the pasture. A farm boy needs to show off his ridin' horse, don't you know.

It seems that those boys are still doing it. Of course, one has to wonder why those reenactments are up there in the treetops instead of down on the ground. Maybe the timber that has grown up in what used to be an open area has simply grown up too thick. It can be tough, horse racing among the trees. And especially so if you've got a horse that won't neck-rein.

Keepin' 'Em Up

Kathrine Mosley of East Liverpool had the darnedest experience after her husband died in the early 1970s.

There had been nothing particularly remarkable about Leonard right up until the day he died. There had been nothing that even suggested that Kathrine would be faced with Leonard hanging around after he was gone.

And, maybe he wasn't hanging around, but there certainly doesn't seem to be any other explanation for what happened in the years following Leonard going to his great reward.

Leonard had always been a neat and shaped-up sort of fellow. He always kept his person, his clothes and his car in tiptop shape. That was just the sort of fellow he was.

After Leonard died, Kathrine just couldn't face the chore of having to clean out his closet. Her having to do that simply seemed like it would be the final and complete recognition that she had lost her husband. It is, of course, understandable why she postponed doing that.

It was about two months after his death when Kathrine found it necessary to go into his closet to search his pockets for a key she needed. She hated to have to do that, but finding that particular key was important, so she made the search.

While she was ratting through those pockets, she couldn't help but notice that his shoes were kind of scruffy.

Kathrine couldn't help but think about how that certainly wasn't something that Leonard would have tolerated. If he had black shoes, they had to be black as black could be, and nice and shiny. If he had brown ones, they had to be nice and brown with no scuff marks visible. That's just the kind of guy Leonard was.

As Kathrine closed that closet door and went back to her duties of the day, she thought about those shoes and how un-Leonard they appeared, having that slightly scruffy sort of look to them.

While Kathrine didn't consciously think about those shoes, that issue must have been working around in the back of her mind.

When the idea came to her that she should get out the shoe polishing kit and shape those shoes up, she almost smiled to herself at the futility of her doing such a thing. She knew that when she did get around to cleaning that closet out, she'd be pitching those shoes and probably most of the others of his effects in there. It certainly wouldn't make any sense to polish a pair of shoes that she would be throwing away anyway.

But those shoes in there were so much at odds with the nature of her husband, she couldn't let go of that issue of their needing a good shining up.

After a couple hours of that stewing around about those shoes, Kathrine dropped what she was doing and hunted down that shoe polishing kit.

She was both kind of embarrassed about what she was about to do and a little irritated with herself for wasting her time and effort. But, at least she'd have that behind her and she could get on with other things.

So, in she marched with that kit and gave those shoes a good shining up. While it was an effort in futility, she did feel better about how the shoes looked when she got done. They definitely had a Leonard Mosley look about them now.

It was about a month later when she finally worked up the mood to clean that closet out. She needed to get rid of all that stuff so she could use the closet for storage.

Armed with some plastic bags to put stuff in, a broom and some dust rags, Kathrine proceeded to get started on that distasteful task.

And, of course, the first thing that caught her eye was that pair of shoes. She was still feeling a little embarrassed about having polished those shoes up, only to pitch them later.

Well, now was the later, and she was going to fill those plastic bags and get shed of all that stuff.

But, she hesitated just a moment as she looked at those shoes. Oddly enough, they were kind of scuffed up, definitely in need of a shine.

That, of course, didn't make any sense. She had gone through all that, yet here they were kind of scruffy as if they had been worn, but not cared for.

When Kathrine picked those shoes up, she was dismayed to find that the lace was badly frayed on the left shoe. She sure hadn't seen that before. In fact, she had never seen a frayed or broken lace on any shoe of Leonard's in all the years they had been married.

That frayed lace really bothered Kathrine. If Leonard were alive to see such a thing, he would have dropped everything so he could get that replaced without delay.

Certainly there was no reason to replace that lace. After all, she was about to pitch those shoes anyway. What difference would it make if they got tossed out with a frayed lace?

Still, it made her anxious about throwing those away in that shape. What would Leonard have thought?

By this time, Kathrine had worked herself into such a state that she could think of dozens of things she would rather do than clean up that closet. Back to the broom closet went the broom and dust rags, and back into the cupboard went the plastic bags. She'd do that job some other time.

When Kathrine went downtown, she had no intention whatsoever to get some new laces. That would have been odd to the point of being unhealthy, and she had no intention of replacing that pair, one of which was frayed.

But there, right there in the store, were some shoelaces right next to another item she had set out to buy that morning.

Somewhat impatiently, Kathrine pitched that little package of shoelaces in with the other things she was buying.

She deliberately chose not to even think about that shoe situation all the way home. It made her uncomfortable, the very idea of replacing those laces. She felt that doing so was bordering on the obsessive, and she really wanted no part of that.

Getting home, she grabbed those laces out of the sack, went in and replaced the laces in those shoes, and went on to other things. She didn't want to think about how silly she had gotten over those shoes.

When Kathrine found a seam on the back of one of those shoes starting to unravel a few weeks later, she was totally mystified. There is no way she would have missed that back seam when she had shined those shoes, but there it was.

How could that be? It was just as if those shoes were starting to wear out. But, shoes just setting in a closet can't wear out..............and they can't get scruffy. Yet these shoes were in need of a polishing job.

Kathrine's concern for her mental well-being led her to sit down and face this issue. Here she had been maintaining a pair of shoes for several weeks now. She had shined them up. She had replaced the laces, and now they needed a shoe repairman's attention. And, besides all that, they were in need of a shine again.

What in the world was going on here?

It was at this point, as she sat there in a chair in the doorway to that closet, that she got to looking at Leonard's other clothes in there. Two of the shirts hanging on that pole were soiled. Both of them looked like they had each been worn two or three times and were in need of some laundering. There is no way in the world that Leonard would have let some dirty shirts hang in his clothes closet. Besides that, Kathrine had hung them there after laundering them before she lost her husband.

It was then that she saw that one of his pairs of trousers was soiled around the bottom of the cuff as if those trousers had been worn and gotten into some dirty water, no doubt from a mud puddle.

Kathrine rose up out of that chair, partly in shock over what she was seeing and partly in order to inspect the clothes in that closet a little more closely.

She found evidence of virtually all of those clothes having been worn since being laundered last. She went through the pockets again and found the most surprising thing of all. She found a receipt for some minor purchase from a store here in East Liverpool. The really odd part of that was that store had not yet been opened for business until after Leonard had died.

The date on that receipt confirmed the impossible. It was the date of Monday……….just last Monday. The receipt was for a carton of an off-brand of cigarettes that Leonard had smoked for a long time.

Then, everything fell into place. The various mysteries associated with that closet that had come up the past few weeks could all be explained if one accepted the fact that Leonard was still using those clothes. He was still using them, getting them dirty and subjecting them to the wear and tear to which clothes falls heir.

Leonard was still with her!

It was Kathrine who reported this story to the author and she also shared the fact that this odd thing continued on until the one year anniversary of his death. After that one year, it was all over.

Kathrine had gotten into the practice of keeping those clothes shipshape. She knew that if he was wearing them, he'd want them to look nice. He was just that sort of fellow, don't you know?

"After that first anniversary of his death, the whole thing stopped. The shoes no longer needed their periodic shining and the clothes no longer got frayed, dirty or used looking."

"What do you suppose that was all about?" I asked.

"I don't really know. I guess he just wanted one more year to sort of wrap things up. Leonard wasn't the kind of person to leave loose ends from his life hanging about.

"Other than that receipt for that carton of cigarettes, I never ran across anything in his pockets that would offer any hint as to what he was doing all day…………..but apparently he was doing something."

So, maybe if you are a button down sort of fellow, you end up with a button down sort of ghost.

One More Game

Jerry Conner was only sixteen, but was the acknowledged number one pitcher in Crestline.

He was a natural on the mound and enjoyed being the best in town.

Folks figured that by the time he was a senior, Crestline would be unstoppable.

Unfortunately, Jerry proved to be very stoppable. He fell victim to a boating accident while on vacation in 1953 and lost his life in that mishap. Jerry Conner would no longer represent the dreams of the fans in Crestline that Crestline would be on the top of the heap in baseball.

The Conner family moved away from Crestline in 1955 and Jerry's friends were pretty much all gone, off to college or off to work somewhere.

By 1962, there was virtually no one left in town who even remembered Jerry............just a few diehard fans of the sport, and a few teachers who had been there when Jerry was in school.

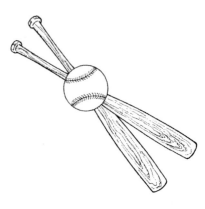

It was in the summer of 1962 when a strange event took place in Crestline.

It was at a ballgame going on. It wasn't an official school function. It wasn't even at the school. It was an improvised game on a vacant lot here in town.

The bases were some gunnysacks half filled with sand that one of the fellows had put together for such occasions.

There had been nothing special in getting that game up................just a few of the fellows passing a summer afternoon away.

They had been into the game for about fifteen minutes when a stranger showed up and asked if he could play, and could he pitch for both sides?

Having a stranger come up and ask to play was not totally unprecedented, but it didn't happen every day, of course.

The really odd thing about this situation was that the fellow was completely suited up, just as if he was playing a game on the high school team.

The fellow who had been approached with this request was so caught by surprise, he simply gave a shrug suggesting approval. The game continued, but with the stranger in the group, a stranger who pitched for both teams.

It didn't take but a few minutes before it was apparent to everybody there that the odd fellow in the uniform was one heck of a great pitcher.

He struck out a number of batters, almost all who went up against him.

As the game went on, fellows became more and more curious about their guest there in that game.

The fellow who had been approached by the lad hadn't gotten a good look at him and had no idea who he was.

By this time, a couple of loafers had stopped to watch the game. These were a couple of old-timers here in Crestline who welcomed the opportunity to have a diversion in what would have otherwise been something of a boring and hot summer day.

One of these two became quite animated as he watched the game, especially as he watched that pitcher.

"Why, that pitcher, the fellow with the uniform on is one good pitcher. Why do you supposed he has a uniform on, playing with a bunch of young bucks in their tee-shirts and jeans?"

His companion neither knew nor cared why that one fellow was wearing a uniform.

"Why, that young man pitches jus' like Todd Conner's boy………..what was his name? He was Todd and Edna Conner's son. He pitches jus' like that Conner kid who was a real good pitcher. Why do you suppose he has a uniform on?"

"I dunno."

All of a sudden the old man rose up off of that park bench. He was going to get some answers to his questions. He was going to get some answers straight from the horse's mouth, so out he went to the pitcher's mound.

To the fellows who had gotten the game up, things were getting odder and odder. Here was this old fellow interrupting their game by walking right out there to the pitcher, obviously to engage the lad in conversation.

As strange as things had gotten, they were about to get a lot stranger within a matter of seconds.

No sooner did that loafer get himself in front of that pitcher, but the old fellow fell to the ground in a heap………..apparently fainting dead away.

That game came to a real fast close as all of the fellows rushed out there to see what the heck was going on.

It was one thing for a couple of loafers to watch their game, but quite another for one of 'em to horn in and interrupt the game by striding out to chat with the pitcher…………and then to fall in a heap like he had a heart attack or something.

The first of the fellows who rushed out there immediately turned his attention to that inert heap on the ground. If that fellow had had a heart attack, he'd probably need help right away.

While his teammate was trying to figure out what was with the old duffer on the ground, the second of the fellows who got to the pitcher's mound was the first one to look directly at the pitcher and up close.

That fellow jumped back in shock when all he saw was a skull within the guy's helmet. It wasn't an image of a skull, like sewn into cloth. It was an actual skull.

Two more of the boys saw that skull also. Then, without warning, it was gone. All that remained was an empty uniform. Nobody was in it or under it as it lay there on the ground next to the old man who, by this time, was starting to come around again.

As the man regained his bearings, he immediately looked around for that pitcher. He rasped out a question, wondering where that skeleton was.

No one in the group had the presence of mind to find a phone and call the police. Everyone was too shocked to even think of that.

In all the turmoil out there at the pitcher's mound, the fellows suddenly realized that empty uniform was no longer there on the ground. No one had left the mound area in the intervening minute or two, yet it was gone……………gone as gone could be.

That incident that day back in 1962 proved to entail a whole lot more questions than it had answers.

Word of the incident made its rounds here in Crestline, especially the part about how that old-timer had recalled that the stranger's pitching style was exactly the same as Jerry Conner's. Folks soon decided that the mysterious disappearing pitcher was, in fact, the ghost of Jerry Conner. It was apparent that the ghost of that lad had come back for one more game.

The old duffer who had set off that strange chain of events by going out to talk to that pitcher swore up and down that the style of that fellow was exactly like that of Jerry Conner, who had been so good and had died in that boating mishap just a few years previously.

There were people in Crestline who hoped for a repeat of that visit from the Conner boy, but it never happened.

Apparently all Jerry wanted was one more game.

The South End Two-Step

Sometimes in doing research for a book of ghost stories, an author will find himself with the distinct feeling he's being scammed.

In fact, this author has pitched out some of the stories he started, convinced that he'd been fed a line of horsehocky. There is no point in laboring over a story that is purely out of someone's imagination, of course.

It becomes a judgmental thing for the author. On occasion, he will find something just too unbelievable.

This writer has some real reservations about this account that he picked up from a fellow warming a barstool in Mansfield. The man seemed to be as sincere as he could be, but you never know.

To back that story up that the barfly recited, the fellow down on the next stool would nod his agreement now and then. Those two were buddies, and those nods of agreement seemed to constitute that other fellow's vouching for the word of his pal.

What qualified that guy on the next stool to testify as to the veracity of the story is something of a good question.

It's a bit of a stretch to believe all this, but it is offered to the reader here.

True or not, here 'tis.

This tale goes back to when Terry Wilcox was a boy on the Wilcox acreage outside of Mansfield back in 1948.

All the critters on an acreage back in the 1930s would be part of a pecking order there on any given place.

The dog occupied the numero uno position there at the Wilcox acreage. It was a good-sized dog, and could even terrorize the horses if he wanted to. So, he was at the top of the heap.

After the dog came the horses, the bull, and so on down through all the pigs and chickens and sheep……….all the way down to the lowest newly-hatched baby chick.

Somewhere in the middle of that structure was a huge old Rock Island Red rooster that wasn't nearly as important as he thought he was.

While most of the animals would accept their position in the pecking order, that rooster was just arrogant enough and just cocky enough that he contested his position all the time. He'd even take on the dog now and then, just to give old Mr. Numero Uno a good pecking on the nose. He'd fly in the faces of the bull and the horses just to show them that they might be higher on the pecking order, but he was still a force to be reckoned with.

While all that might seem to be an odd thing to a city slicker, it's simply a fact of life on an acreage, and drives a lot of things like who gets to eat first, who gets to lie in that cozy little corner soaking up the early spring warmth, etc.

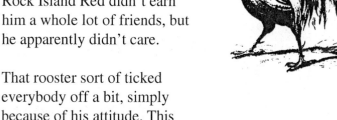

That contentious nature of that Rock Island Red didn't earn him a whole lot of friends, but he apparently didn't care.

That rooster sort of ticked everybody off a bit, simply because of his attitude. This led the dog to yank a feather or two out now and then just for the heck of it. When the horses could get that rooster positioned just right behind them, they'd let fly with a kick that'd send that cocky rooster through the air to a painful landing somewhere else.

Terry Wilcox, being a human being, was outside of the whole pecking order thing, but he pretty much shared a level of distain for that rooster. He had his own ways of hassling that ball of feathered egotism.

There was a situation there among the chickens that provided Terry a really unique way to hassle that rooster. That was the molting thing. Molting is a phase that chickens will go through in the summer. Among the physiological effects of molting is that the feathers tend to drop off the south ends of chickens when they molt.

Those chickens would have to go through the humility of walking around the place with bare bottoms. To make it even more humiliating, those bare bottoms would tend to get sunburned.

Can you just imagine what it must be like to……………..well, we best not get into all that.

Anyway, those chickens had to go through that simply because they were chickens. And that cocky Rhode Island Red rooster was no exception.

It's kind of hard to maintain one's dignity when one's south end is bare and sunburned, but that rooster gave it the old college try.

Being in that delicate condition, that old rooster was particularly vulnerable to a little trick that Terry had come up with.

Country boys, back then, all enjoyed a series of weapons they would use for one fun thing or another. As they got older, they could graduate from slingshots and BB guns to a real gun............a .22 rifle.

And Terry had one. He used it to plink targets, get a rabbit now and then, and for general terrorizing purposes.

It was that .22 that provided Terry with a really unique way to hassle that snotty rooster.

He found out that if he could catch a chicken over there in the area of the barn lot that had some gravel in it, he could carefully shoot his .22 so the bullet would hit the ground right under the chicken. That bullet would kick up a few little pieces of gravel.

Those little hunks of gravel would take off in all directions. It was the ones that went straight up that would offer the most fun.

Those little missiles going straight up at a high speed would often impact on the chicken...........right on that bare bottom - very often a sunburned bottom.

That, in turn, would move that chicken to go through all kinds of gyrations.

A country boy had to take his amusements where he could, of course. And Terry found the squawking and flapping that would ensue well worth the cost of a .22 shell.

As much fun as all that was for Terry, it was especially fun to pull that on that snotty rooster.

Pulling that trick off required everything to fall into place. It necessitated a bare bottomed chicken and one in an area of the barn lot where there was some gravel.

The trick required that the bullet hit the ground in just the right place. And, of course, it was important for that bullet not to wend its way through the chicken, proper. A country boy can get in lots of trouble for killing a Sunday dinner on the hoof.

It was on a hot Saturday afternoon when Terry found things falling into place perfectly. He had his .22 with him and there was that cocky old Rock Island Red right out there in the gravel portion of the barn lot.

The rooster was molting, so was vulnerable to Terry's bullet-between-the-legs trick.

Terry got himself positioned where he could do his little thing. The rooster was facing the lad, but that was no problem. All he had to do was plant that bullet right between the legs of that rooster, and he'd launch that snotty rooster from where he stood, probably all the way over toward the corncrib.

It was at that crucial point, and Terry had his .22 up and ready to fire.

Old Mr. Rooster was gazing out across the barn lot, undoubtedly thinking about where to find a nice fat June bug.

Apparently a delicious looking bug showed up right there in front of that Rock Island Red.

Hang in there, the ghost part is coming up.

Terry didn't know it, but things were falling into place that he would have years to regret.

Terry's finger was tightening on the trigger and that rooster was just a couple of seconds away from one stung south end.

Terry was only a second or two away from the opportunity to see that snotty rooster about go into orbit.

Just as that finger tightened to that critical point, Old Mr. Rooster chose to gather up that bug there in front of him.

Down went that head to claim that prize, and off went that bullet, bound for that gravel between the rooster's legs.

That bullet was well aimed and found the exact spot Terry was aiming for…………unfortunately just a millisecond after taking a side trip through that rooster's head.

There was no launching off toward the corncrib. All there was was one decided slump to the ground and one dead rooster.

Terry was shocked at that turn of events. He sure hadn't meant to do in that rooster, but he did.

As far as Terry was concerned, the story was all over. And, most certainly, it was over for that rooster.

Oops, not quite.

It wasn't but a couple of nights later that Terry was layin' in bed asleep. Suddenly he woke up with the distinct feeling that something was amiss.

And, there sure was something amiss. Right there on the foot of the bed's framework was perched a huge old Rock Island Red rooster. It looked like most other Rock Island Reds, except Terry could see right through the critter.

Now, the writer isn't going to accept responsibility for a kid seeing the ghost of a chicken. But that was what was obviously going on.

Apparently the rooster wasn't a bit happy about being done in by the kid, and was back to hassle him.

And, hassle him he did for years. Every now and then, Terry would wake up in the middle of the night and have to face a spook chicken there on the end of his bed.

That spook never seemed to offer to give Terry any problem. He was just there.

After a few years of finding a ghost chicken on the foot of your bed is problem enough.

Terry's problem persisted for the rest of his life until his death in 2003.

We don't know, of course, if Terry and that chicken have crossed paths in the land of eternity. Perhaps that rooster is still mad at Terry Wilcox. We just don't know.

25% Off

Elmer Roper, from out along 58, between Ashland and Nankin, kind of got left out when they passed out the milk of human kindness. The man had no understanding of, nor any interest in the problems that others had. Unless something affected him, it simply didn't exist.

Elmer's lack of compassion for his fellow humans was more than made up for by his riches. The man had far more money than what was good for him.

Elmer didn't let his money lay around. He worked it just as hard as he worked the people who had the misfortune to be his employees.

While Elmer had a number of enterprises going on, the one he liked most was his lending service. He charged his customers 25% of the principal as annual interest. Old Elmer pretty much set the standard for hosing folks over pretty bad. Of course, he hadn't reduced his lending practices and abuse of his customers to a fine art, like the credit card companies were to do later, but he did a pretty good job for an amateur. He did well enough that he made lots of money with his lending business.

His entrapment of Levi Caldwell into years of indebtedness was something he was to eventually learn to wish he hadn't done.

That Levi Caldwell thing all started out with a loan for some livestock and grew into a situation in which Levi found himself getting deeper and deeper into debt.

Levi made every effort to get out from under that undesirable situation, but never did. He died still owing Elmer quite a bit of money.

Those IOUs Elmer had with Levi's signatures on them enabled him to scoop up every last shred of what little Levi had left when he died.

Elmer came out of that deal smelling like a rose, and cared not a whit that Levi had moved on to his rewards. He simply didn't care what happened to the man.

But, Elmer was shortly to learn to care a lot about the fate of Levi Caldwell.

It was about a week after Levi's death when Elmer was out in his hog house doing his chores out there, and seeing to twelve hogs he had just purchased. Wouldn't you know it, but several of those hogs had taken sick and looked like they had been drug through a knothole.

Elmer's first reaction to seeing those hogs in their condition was to blurt out his feelings.

"Oh, I sure hope I don't lose any of those hogs. They cost me more than I want to remember."

No sooner had he gotten that out of his mouth when he heard a voice………..

"Okay, but it'll cost you 25 percent."

Elmer straightened up in a hurry. He sure wasn't accustomed to hearing voices coming down out of the rafters about anything………..much less the cost of his wishes coming true.

Elmer walked all over there inside the hog house in an attempt to find the source of that voice. All he found was the dust always so thick in such structures, and a bunch of hogs that apparently could care less about voices coming out of nowhere that way.

All that was in vain. He found no hint at all about where that voice had come from, or whose voice it was.

Meanwhile, having some of those new hogs taking sick was far too serious for him to be off chasing voices somewhere. He needed to tend to those sick animals.

Elmer had some medicine that he stuffed down those hogs, hoping for the best.

The best didn't happen. Three of those hogs went to that great mud hole in the sky within forty-eight hours.

Mmmmmmmmmmmmmmmmm……………that was three hogs out of the twelve. Three out of twelve………… It didn't take Elmer long to do the math. He had up and lost 25% of that bunch of new hogs.

And that voice had said that it'd cost him 25%. That, of course, was the same 25% that Elmer had been charging interest on his loans.

Elmer didn't put two and two together to figure things out at that time, but he would.

It wasn't but a couple of days later when he was in town, running some errands, when he heard there had been a small tornado out east of town.

Since Elmer lived out that way, it didn't take him long to scurry out to his place to check things out. He had always been concerned about tornadoes, and the last thing he needed was to have one mess things up out there.

As he aimed his old pickup down that gravel that led out to his place, he got more and more worried as he saw increasing evidence of some serious damage to a couple places there along the road.

"Man, I sure hope that storm didn't touch down there at the house!"

He didn't have anyone with him in that pickup, but still gave voice to his worries simply as a matter of habit.

No sooner had he gotten that out of his mouth when he heard a voice:

"Okay, but it'll cost you twenty-five percent."

Elmer straightened up in a hurry. He sure wasn't accustomed to hearing voices coming down out of the space there in his pickup. But there was that voice again.

There he was – all alone there in that truck, and didn't have a radio in it, so it couldn't have been a voice from the radio.

He was going down that road about fifty miles an hour, with the windows rolled up, so it wasn't a voice that could have come into the cab of that truck from outside.

This time was a tad different, though. This time Elmer thought that the voice had a familiar ring to it. But he still couldn't figure out whose it was, or how that voice rang out in the first place.

And that part about it'd cost him 25%. 25% of what? Might it mean 25% of the house?

That thought was pretty alarming since the last time he heard that, it was just after he had said something to himself out loud, and just before he lost 25% of his new bunch of hogs.

Did that mean he'd be losing part of his house?

Coming over that little rise just before getting to the house was all it took to answer some of those questions for Elmer.

That twister had indeed touched down there at his place. He could see right off that the garden was in shambles, and one clothesline pole was broken off.

But, the real bad news was the house. Most of it was still intact, but the whole back end of the house was gone! It was the new part he had added just recently.

That new addition was entirely gone, leaving only the foundation and a few strewn-around pieces of debris were all that was left.

A recollection of that voice came back to Elmer.

"Yeah, but it'll cost you 25%."

Elmer sat there – with the engine still running. He had added that 600-square-foot addition onto his house, giving him a nice comfortable 2400 square feet. That meant that 25% of his home was gone.

Since Elmer didn't believe in having insurance, that loss would be coming right out of his pocket.

Then it hit him. He knew that voice. That was Levi Caldwell's voice. Both times that voice had had a little lilt at the end of the sentence. That was the way Levi had always talked!

But, Levi was dead. Elmer had good reason to know that fact, since he ended up with all of Levi's worldly goods.

The mystery was over. Elmer knew full well what was going on. Levi Caldwell was haunting him and doing so in a terribly painful way. He was visiting disasters on him, disasters that caused him to lose 25% of something or other. First, it was his hogs, then his house.

But, apparently Levi wasn't done. Elmer ended up with only 25% of a crop by the time some hail got done with him. The neighbors didn't get that hail, but Elmer sure did.

Then things got serious. Elmer had long been diabetic, and that disease progressed to the point that some of both legs had to be amputated.

The doctors told Elmer that they didn't know how much they'd have to take. They told him they'd do what they could and take no more than necessary.

"Well, Doc, I know how much you'll have to take. I weigh 180 pounds, so you'll need to take 45 pounds of my legs."

The doctors' questioning looks led Elmer to tell them that they would end up taking 25% of his body.

And Elmer went on to explain about his losses of 25% of anything since he was being haunted by the ghost of a man he had lent money to for a return of 25%.

The doctors gave Elmer disapproving looks as only doctors can do.

Those were really surprised doctors when they discovered that Elmer was right on. They removed a full twenty-five percent of his body that day.

Elmer's losses continued.

His ultimate loss was in 1994 when he was diagnosed with a terminal problem. His doctor estimated that Elmer had two months to live.

Alarmed, Elmer said, "Only six weeks, Doc?"

"Well, I said two months, but……………….."

"It'll be a fourth less than that, Doc. I figure I'll be gone in six weeks."

Six weeks later, Elmer joined Levi.

The Handyman

Some folks shouldn't get married. That is, they shouldn't get married to each other.

Robert and Eunice Tobbins of Delphos were two such people. They might well have been okay for other spouses, but they sure weren't for each other. They ended up being the two most argumentative people around. They would argue over anything. If there wasn't something to argue about, they'd figure out something.

Those two argued every day of their married life............well, almost. The first three or four days they got along pretty well, but it all went downhill from there.

It wasn't a matter of little spats. It didn't take long for those two to discover that they didn't love each other, after all. Fact is, they didn't even like each other.

Like others who engage in confrontation over a long period of time, the Tobbins had a specialty.

Their specialty was to claim to be the cause of each other's trials and tribulations. That way, when they would argue, each could have the satisfaction of claiming to be the source of the other's discomforts.

For example, if Robert stubbed his toe, Eunice would be sure he understood that that sore toe was her doing because she had left the offending object out in the way. It didn't make a toe feel any better when there was someone there who would rush in to claim responsibility for its injury.

And, Eunice couldn't catch a cold without Robert laying claim to having left the bedroom window cracked open there on her side of the bed. There is nothing like a good old draft on a person to get a cold going good, you know.

Fortunately, that scrapping pair never had any children. Of course, one can't help but to speculate as to why they remained childless.

All that scrapping and angry tirades came to an end in 1972 when Robert up and died. The only reason those two didn't argue about the cause of death was because Robert wasn't in any condition to hold up his end of an argument. Had he been able to do that, Eunice would have been more than willing to argue about that. And, no doubt he'd been more than willing to fuss over that if he could have.

Robert's death had impacts on Eunice's life beyond simply bringing all the arguing to a close. She had worked on and off for several years, but she found it necessary to work full time after he died.

She found a factory job in Lima. That necessitated her driving to Lima every weekday from where she lived in Delphos.

That situation and the need for someone to do some fix-up work around the house led her to end up hiring a handyman without ever having the opportunity to see him. They did all their correspondence by telephone since he was from out of town and couldn't come to Delphos on weekends when Eunice was home.

Eunice had heard about this fellow and how he did odd jobs. A couple of phone calls and he was hired to do a number of odd jobs there at Eunice's place.

And they'd leave each other notes. If it wasn't a note from him about his needing for her to call the lumberyard to order some materials, it'd be her instructing him to set that new window in the kitchen so it'd be centered on the wall instead of offset like the old one had been.

Eunice was happy with this fellow's work and he was affordable, so that business of his doing odd jobs for her continued for quite a while.

Eunice seemed to be plagued by ill fortune over a number of things during the period of time. It all started out small. When she got home after her handyman had installed a new cabinet, she ended up breaking off a fingernail when she opened the door to see how it was going to work for her.

That was a painful injury, one that was undoubtedly due to her own carelessness. The man hadn't installed that cabinet in such a way that it would have injured Eunice, but that's what it ended up doing.

Then the new linoleum he had put down in the bathroom was a vast improvement in appearance over what had been there. But, wouldn't you know it………..she hadn't been in that bathroom but a few times when she slipped on that new floor and got a good black eye when her face hit the little chair she had in front of the mirror.

That wasn't the man's fault, of course. She had picked that linoleum out and she knew when she got it that it was going to be glossy, so it'd probably be slick.

During the course of their telephone conversations, Eunice shared accounts of her misfortunes with her handyman. She didn't do that because she held him responsible, but only did so as a matter of interest.

It was one such mishap after the other for the poor girl, and she began to think that she never would get over her run of bad luck.

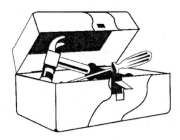

That whole cozy arrangement came to an end one day when she was telling her handyman about how she had stubbed her toe on his toolbox he had out there in the garage. Apparently she had sandals on or some other shoe that offered her no protection at all, and she ended up with a rather severe injury from that little mishap.

As she told her helper about this over the phone, with some observation that struck Eunice as being an odd thing to say. She couldn't put her finger on it, but there was something about that response that had a familiar ring to it.

Eunice would have forgotten that incident, but it kept nagging at her. Not only was it an odd response, but she couldn't help but to think that she had heard that line before, and within the context of a toe-stubbing incident.

That night she was almost asleep when it suddenly all came back to her. She sat up in bed wide awake with shock.

She recalled that sentence from an earlier time. It was one that she had shot at Robert that time he had stubbed his toe. It was a line she came up with that had been designed to show how she could have cared less what had happened to his stupid old toe. It had also been designed to convey to him that she could lay claim for being the cause of that toe-stubbing incident.

That was the same sentence she had heard before! And, she had good reason to know exactly how that sentence went, and how it was designed to hurt. After all, it was her line, so she had good reason to recall it.

While she hadn't picked up on how that response from her handyman could have meant to hurt, she came to the conclusion that it had been. As she sat there in her bed, she couldn't help but think about how a statement she had made that was meant to hurt had come back to her. And, as she thought about it, she realized that the handyman's response did hurt her, indeed. It suggested a lack of concern on his part over her mishap.

Eunice couldn't believe what she got to speculating over. She couldn't believe that she was mulling over the possibility that her husband had come back to hassle her..........or, at least the ghost of her husband was back.

Eunice sat there and realized that she had never seen the man, and how it was odd that they never had been able to meet. The one weekday when she found it possible to be home, her handyman had suddenly discovered that he couldn't work that day. As she thought about all that, she recognized that there had been other times when they could have met that they didn't because of some last minute conflict that he came up with.

Was he really avoiding her? Was he really the ghost of her husband out to engineer a bunch of injuries for her that he could enjoy having been the cause?

Eunice still hadn't figured out what to do about the whole situation by the next morning when she got a call from her handyman to discuss some detail on some work he was going to be doing that week. It was some work on the replacement of some additional windows.

That's when the idea came to her. She knew that Robert had been burdened with an ever-so-slight speech impediment. She knew he couldn't get his tongue around the word "aluminum." All the time they had been married, he never could pronounce that word.

"Aluminum" is not a word that a person can substitute another word for, so when Robert had been forced to use the word, he'd butcher it up and move on.

Eunice saw this as her opportunity. She got to discussing windows and the options that were available to her.

She came up with a line in which she recited the options – those being wood, vinyl and the other one. She struggled with trying to find the word for that third kind of window frame. She knew that her handyman would know that the third kind of window was aluminum, and she figured she could force him to use the word.

The man tried to avoid the use of that word, but she wouldn't let it go. She pressed him to help her think of that word, so he pretty much had to use that awful word "aluminum."

And, he butchered it up.

Robert wasn't the only man in the world who had had trouble with that word, but his messing it up when he tried to use it was unique to him. He put a twist to it that was truly different.

And, that's exactly the way the handyman said it.

It was at that point that Eunice realized what had been going on. She knew then that Robert was back. She knew he was back and he was causing her all kinds of trouble. It was because of him that she had suffered that broken nail, that black eye and that severely-stubbed toe. She knew that those were merely some of the injuries she had had to put up with lately.

And, they were all his fault!

Eunice had plans on sneaking home to finally meet her "handyman" while he was working on her place, and wouldn't be expecting her to come home.

But, she didn't have the willpower not to get into an argument with the man right there over the telephone. During the course of that argument, it was clear that Eunice was on to him.

The telephone suddenly went silent, and all Eunice could hear was a dial tone.

She never heard from her handyman again. She had run up a bill with him, but he never showed up to collect. Apparently ghosts don't need money.

The Worn Spot

Everyone has been in one of those little diners where Mom and Pop have spent their lifetimes providing their customers with their many rations of bacon and eggs, and with their coffee and juice.

Over the years, those establishments often become something of a family with the regulars showing up sure as the sun rises in the east.

And, of course, there is the situation that always accompanies such situations. That is that certain of the regulars will always sit on certain stools.

The whole process is not a whole lot unlike the order of things in an old-fashioned milking barn. Each cow had her place and would religiously occupy that particular place.

And, part of a diner doing its thing would be the wearing away of the design on the Formica countertop in front of each stool.

The little diner in Beaverdam had all that going on. Most of those regulars had their stool they'd warm up each morning. That fellow who always sat in the second stool from the end could have found his coffee just as good were he to sit on the third stool, or even the fourth, or the fifth. But, he wouldn't do that. It was always the second stool for him.

And, that fellow who kept stool number seven warm would not have dreamt of sitting on a different one.

Like other regulars, Clark Manning had his favorite, also. It was the one that happened to be the exact center one. Clark probably wasn't aware that his stool was the exact center one. It was just the stool he headed for each morning. His feet probably would have taken him to that stool were he to have entered the diner blindfolded.

And, like every other point on that long counter, there was a worn spot on that Formica right in front of Clark's stool.

The pattern on that countertop was an image of oak boards. But, it was only an image, and everyone knew it was only an image. As the Formica would wear away there at each place, the underlying white would show through.

Clark had, through the years, contributed to that wearing away of the Formica surface, as had other customers before him. And, of course, there would be others during the course of the day who would occupy his spot when he was off to work.

That is, Clark contributed to that wearing away of that countertop until he died in 1962.

Like every other "family," the death of Clark was mourned by the Landers who ran the diner, as well as the other regulars there in that diner.

While the Landers were getting ready to do some remodeling in the diner, it had nothing to do with Clarks' death. They just happened to be doing that about the time Clark went to his reward.

Part of that remodeling involved a number of things that had an impact on the counter areas. For one thing, they moved the cash register from the back bar out onto the counter itself. They ended up with that cash register right smack in the center of the counter, thus rendering Clarks' place unusable. They took up the stool, leaving a gap there, thus making room for the cash register there on the counter.

That remodeling elicited lots of comments from the regulars, of course. More than one of them voiced concerns about what Clark was going to do since his stool was gone, and there was no longer "Clark's place."

But, of course, all that was in jest. Clark was gone, and would have no real concerns about "his place" there in that little diner anymore. He had his place out at the cemetery now, and things were different.

Beneath the cash register was a little cubbyhole created when that cash register was rigged up to be a few inches off the top of the counter itself.

The Landers found that little cubbyhole to be a handy place for keeping rolls of paper for the cash register, the money bags for stocking the register each day with the appropriate change and so forth.

That little cubbyhole hardly ever saw the light of day, much less the wear and tear of being used as an eating surface.

During meal times, that countertop had a lot going on it, but not in that little cubbyhole. It was strictly for the storage of stuff.

Lots of years went by and lots of plates of bacon and eggs got shoved across the counter in that little diner.

Meanwhile, a photo of the interior of that diner got uncovered from a junk drawer, and found itself framed and hung on the wall.

That photo earned itself lots of discussion among the Landers and the regulars. Any number of times, folks would run their fingers over the glass covering the photo as people would reminisce about how things were way back in the early sixties.

Both the Landers were still working off and on in the diner by 1984, but the management of the place had pretty much been turned over to their daughter, Laura, and her husband.

That whole gang and some of the customers were oohing and ahhing over that photo when it was first put up.

It was Laura who saw that one of the old regulars, Clark Manning, was there in that photo.

Laura delighted in noticing something about Clark that most of the folks had forgotten about. Clark had a habit of eating with his right hand and resting his left elbow on the countertop so he could use that left forearm and hand to wave around as he made various political and social observations there from that center stool.

So, in addition to the worn spot created by the plate and silverware, Clark's spot sported an extra worn spot, one created by that elbow always resting there to the left of his plate.

Others then recalled how Clark had done that, all of which brought out lots of giggling about how those old-timers all had their little habits.

That reminiscing had to take a backseat as the business picked up that morning and folks went back to their stools or back to their chores.

It turned out to be a busy day, an inopportune day for the fellow from the cash register company to come to do some repair work on that machine. But, the man showed up, so Laura had to work out of a cigar box while the fellow peered into the machine's innards to figure out a problem.

Whatever the problem was, it was one that necessitated taking the cash register clear out to get into it properly.

For the first time in twenty years, that counter space in front of what had been Clark's stool saw the full light of day.

Laura grabbed up a bar rag as soon as the man lifted up the register. She knew there'd be a twenty-year accumulation of dust and grime under there, and she sure didn't want the customers sitting around getting a glimpse of that. She knew she'd get all kinds of static over her poor housekeeping if all that dirt showed itself.

The man just got turned around with that cash register so he could haul it over to a table where he could work on it. He just got turned around when Laura swooped down with her trusty bar rag to get that dirt wiped up.

Laura also expected to see the counter totally without a worn spot on it since it had been tucked away all those years. Elsewhere that "new" counter was showing its age pretty much.

Several of the fellows there, loitering over a cup of coffee, saw the odd sight of Laura standing there with a bar rag in her hand and a shocked look on her face.

Laura had good reason to be shocked at that tucked away space that had served no purpose for twenty years other than that of hiding some rolls of cash register paper and stored some change bags.

That rectangular area under that cash register wasn't at all dirty. Her resolve to wipe that area clean was quite pointless. There was no dirt to clean up.

There was no way that could be……….but it was.

But, the surprises weren't over with.

There on that surface, that surface that hadn't had things rubbed over it for twenty years, had the worn appearance so common to diner countertops.

There was that worn spot there, just about like the others on that twenty-year-old "new" countertop. Not one single meal had been eaten there. Not one coffee cup had rested on that surface. Yet there was that worn spot.

Laura's gasp of surprise is what alerted that morning's collection of diners to get up and come over there to see what the excitement was all about.

The attention paid to that situation rivaled that occasioned by the earlier hanging of that photo that had showed the interior of that diner of a lot of years earlier.

The lack-of-dust situation was surprising enough, but that worn spot was a total mystery.

It was Saul Cummins who first noticed the thing that both deepened the mystery of the situation as it also offered an explanation for it.

That worn spot had something different about it. It had its own little twist that made a couple of the fellows step back just a pace when Saul made his observation.

There, just to the left of the plates' worn spot was another smaller one. It was a little round worn spot, just like the one Clark had worn in that earlier counter all those years earlier.

As Laura and those customers stood there contemplating that worn spot, it became apparent to all of them that Clark Manning was still a regular there in that little diner. He might have died twenty years earlier, but he was still a regular.

Clark must still have kept his interest in politics and such since he had still apparently been gyrating that left arm around to emphasize a point he'd make in those discussions that never took place.

The Return Of The Ring

Everything was quite hunky-dory when Graham Meaker gave Darlene Wallis that beautiful diamond ring, an engagement ring that foretold a wedding that was supposed to happen the following November.

Like virtually all newly-engaged couples, those two were knock-your-socks-off crazy in love with each other. Theirs was the romance of the century, and all that stuff that romance would withstand the passing of a million years, or the total annihilation of the universe. It was forever and ever, and would survive anything at all.

That is, anything but the arrival of Brad Cole there in Massillon.

Brad was a whole lot less than the passage of an eternity or the annihilation of the universe, but he was more than enough to shoot Graham right out of the saddle in that timeless romance with Darlene.

Needless to say, all that was a severe disappointment to Graham, having a total stranger move into town and ending his red hot romance that way.

So Graham had no choice but to move on.

Prior to moving on, however, he decided it'd be just fine to get that diamond back.

While Darlene no longer had any interest in Graham, she had developed a real attachment to that ring. It was a really expensive ring, and Darlene saw that thing as a ticket for her to buy something she wouldn't have been able to afford otherwise.

"No, Graham. I'm keeping it."

That didn't set well with Graham at all.

As it turned out, Graham spent the next year and a half of his life in a vain attempt to recover that ring. It also turned out that he spent the rest of his life in that attempt, for he died just a year and a half after Brad came to town and shot him out of the saddle.

We don't know how Graham died, but he did.

That, of course, left Darlene off the hook. She no longer had to put up with that Meaker lad, hounding her for that ring………..the ring that was rightfully hers since he had given it to her.

Other than feeling a sense of relief from not having to get hassled by Graham, that spoiled brat felt nothing about the death of her boyfriend of a couple years earlier.

So much for eternities and the annihilation of the universe.

Darlene didn't even bother to attend the funeral. She and Fred were having way too much fun in their romance.

Yeah, I know……………..who's Fred?

Fred was the guy who replaced Dennis who replaced Roger who replaced Brad………the original shooter out of the saddle.

That string of boyfriends came and went, but Darlene still had that nice diamond ring. She hadn't decided yet what sort of goodie she was going to enjoy at the expense of that poor fellow occupying a casket in the cemetery.

Just to be sure it was nice and safe, Darlene would check the bottom of that second bureau drawer where she kept that ring. It was always setting in there, waiting for whatever goodie she was going to come up with to purchase with that ring.

That is, it was always in that little corner of that second drawer until one day it turned up missing. It was just plain missing. There was no evidence of a robbery or anything. It was just missing.

Darlene turned that bureau drawer about inside out in her search for that ring, as well as the other drawers in that bureau, but still no ring.

Darlene searched and searched on that awful day when she discovered the ring was missing, as well as many other times, but it never turned up.

While Darlene couldn't find the ring, it found her. She started to have visits in the night…………visits of the ghost of Graham. He would show up standing in her bedroom, always with that ring held out so it would catch any stray moonlight or starlight, making it glitter and shine as only a diamond ring can do.

Sometimes Darlene would hear a subdued little cough, wake up and see that ghost of Graham. She knew it was a ghost for she could see right through him. He appeared as more of an image simply suspended in the air, not real distinct. But, he was distinct enough that she knew who he was. And, he'd always be holding one hand out to her, a hand holding that ring.

This whole thing wore heavily on Darlene. Those carefree days of endless boyfriends became a thing of the past. Darlene found her tormentor had driven off all those girlish pleasures she had known, and she found the years weighing heavily on her shoulders.

Those years also had their way out there in that cemetery. That little creek had grown into a larger and more menacing thing, and ended up eroding the ground away out from several of the caskets it that ground.

Graham's was one of them. In the fall into the creek, his casket broke open enough that it had to be repaired in order to properly contain the dust and now-rotten clothes contained within that casket.

It was during that repair work that the workmen there in the cemetery found something of a surprise.

They found a diamond ring clutched in the lifeless hands of Graham Meaker…………the ring he had given to Darlene Wallis all those years earlier.

Pickled Liver

Steve Dickerson left home as soon as he could. He left as soon as he was old enough to support himself, doing odd jobs in Canton.

It didn't take a whole lot to feed, house and clothe a young fellow who was more than willing to live cheap for the privilege of escaping his home.

Maybe he left sooner than he should have, but he simply couldn't wait to get out from under his tyrannical father.

Old Man Dickerson enjoyed all the prescribed activities appropriate for a terrible parent. He sort of specialized in wife beating, whupping up on the kids for little or no reason, and exhibiting financial responsibility by properly dividing his assets among a variety of things...............things like booze, stud poker and ladies of questionable character.

Somehow Steve and his siblings survived their childhoods and grew into responsible adults. That, of course, certainly wasn't Old Man Dickerson's fault.

Maybe that suggests that providing kids with a good solid bad example can be as effective as a good example.

Old Man Dickerson had gathered up an assortment of mementos from his various exploits. These included a couple of disfigured fingers, a long purple scar across his cheek and a .38 bullet lodged between a couple of ribs.

That old fellow was actually proud of his reminders of a life of debauchery and uselessness. That is, he was proud of all those except for that piece of lead lodged between those two ribs. That thing would give him some good sharp pains whenever he'd exert himself. That bullet proved to be something that would often be a reminder of the kind of life he led.

It wasn't very often that any of those kids would ask their father for anything. Such requests were usually simply opportunities for the old man to dole out another portion of either verbal abuse or physical abuse. Often times the old man would, when asked a favor, tell the kid that the only thing he'd give 'em was that .38 slug he was carrying around.

That intelligent response to requests for favors could just about be depended on. It was just kind of a stock answer.

None of the kids ever suggested out loud that the old man deserved all the aches and pains he got from that .38 slug that he got. Even children can become hardened with such upbringing.

It was a number of years after Steve left home that his father finally achieved his drinking himself to death. The doctor's technical term for it was "pickled liver."

By this time the remaining children had all left home, all going their separate ways, each one as eager as the last to get out from under his or her oppressive father.

And, by this time, Steve had worked himself up the ladder nicely. His odd jobs he took on when he had first left home evolved into a steady job where he rose through the ranks to become a person of rather significant responsibility. He took some classes, and eventually won certification as a CPA. It was in that capacity as a CPA where he rose even further up the ladder to become a corporate exec.

Along the way, Steve provided help for his mother and a couple of his siblings.

Steve, as well as the other children, all gathered at their mother's home for the occasion of the burial of that victim of pickled liver. None of them cared one way or the other about the fate of their father, but they gathered at the funeral for the sake of their mother.

One benefit that Old Man Dickerson's death was to provide his family a chance for the rest of them to get together to celebrate something.

Lots of visiting got done, lots of memories recalled and lots of good eats got eaten as the children and their mother recalled incidents from all those years earlier.

It was the day after all that carryings-on when Steve developed a distinct pain in his chest.

He feared the worst, of course, and hoped that it was nothing more serious than his responding to something he ate at that funeral.

The doctor's theory was that Steve was just falling victim to his advancing years, but suggested they do some tests to confirm or deny that.

So, lots of tests got run, and Steve found himself back in the doctor's office to get the word on what ailed him.

The doctor appeared a bit perplexed when he sat down with Steve to talk about the outcome of the tests.

"I didn't realize, Steve, you had been in combat, but you're carrying a souvenir from that. We can go in and remove that bullet from your chest wall."

"Bullet?"

"Yeah, Steve, you've got a bullet lodged there between a couple of ribs. It appears that it has been there for a while. I'm surprised you didn't realize you had that. You were in combat in the service, right?"

No, Steve wasn't in combat. He wasn't even in the service…………..and no, it would be impossible for him to be packing around any lead from any gunplay.

All that left the doctor a bit confused as to how Steve might have ended up with a bullet in him. But, he was confident that he was right. He even gave Steve a little jab in the side to demonstrate how that bullet was there, and how it could be felt. Just to confirm all that, the doctor broke out the x-rays to show Steve the bullet. The x-ray tech had taken pictures of it from a couple of different angles, and there was no question as to what it was.

As the doctor was droving on about this, and as Steve was looking at those x-rays, his mind went back to his childhood when his useless old man would offer to give his kids that bullet between his ribs if they wanted any kind of favor from him.

But, there was no way that could have happened, of course. A fellow doesn't go belly-up and bequeath a bullet lodged in him on to his children or anybody else. All that was was just talk. But, how could Steve have that bullet there within his own chest wall?

CPAs usually don't lead the kind of life that results in their engaging in just a whole lot of gunplay. And, Steve knew he'd never been in a gunfight in his life. He supposed that maybe he had been hit by a stray bullet, and hadn't even felt it, but that didn't make much sense either.

Until the doctor could make arrangements for the surgery, all Steve had on his hands was a mystery.

The operation got done, and that object was removed. There it had laid, lodged between the second and third ribs on his left side.

And, sure enough, it was a bullet………and sure enough, a .38 caliber bullet. And, there it was, right where Old Man Dickerson had packed his hardware around, hardware he would offer to share with his children.

Apparently the old man was able to pull that off.

Apparently, he was able to do, as a ghost, what he couldn't do while he was in the process of pickling his liver.

The Inconvenience

When Ben and Alice bought that old brick house, they neither knew nor cared about the history of the place. All they knew was that the price was right, and it would make one heck of a nice B&B.

It was a fixer-upper without a doubt, and would involve a lot of work to bring it up to a quality appropriate for a B&B. Still, they thought it was the opportunity of a lifetime.

So, this couple bought the old Victorian mansion, and started down the long road of repairing it and restoring its 1800's beauty.

Ok, I'm lying about this being appropriate for this book. The circumstances detailed in this story didn't happen near here at all. This story really comes to us from London, Kentucky, on I-75.

But, I'm putting this story in this book anyway because it's such a good one. What I'm depending on is that the reader won't read this little bitty print in this footnote...or if he does, that he'll forgive my transgression in putting this story in this book.

Thanks for your indulgence.

In order to save money, the couple decided to live in the place while they were doing the refurbishing. During the course of their work, they found out a bit of the history of the place as they would visit with the neighbors.

The fact that it had been a house of ill repute back in the 1800s didn't really make any difference to them. After almost a hundred years of the house having been a private residence, neither Ben nor Alice expected anyone to confuse their new place with a house of ill repute.

The work progressed slowly as it always does when you are trying to bootstrap a project.

And, of course, there were any number of times that problems arose that gave them second thoughts about the wisdom of doing the project.

It was Ben who was most easily discouraged by the setbacks they would encounter.

Alice, on the other hand, was more inclined to take the long view, and to realize that when they got done with it, it would be a beautiful place, well worth the time and money to make it all happen.

During each of those times that Ben would question if they should continue, Alice would counter with her standard answer...
"It'll all work out alright."

Ben could just about depend on hearing that...

"It'll all work out alright" whenever he'd suggest they sell the place, and move on.

Then, one night, an event took place that changed everything. It was after a hard day's work that Ben had gone to bed early. He was bushed, and all he wanted to do was hit the sack and get some sleep.

He had just crawled into bed, fluffed his pillow up to his liking and closed his eyes.

Suddenly, as he laid there on his side ready to go to sleep, he felt someone get into bed with him. This sort of surprised Ben because Alice had, just a few minutes earlier, told him that she was going to stay up and put one more coat of varnish on some woodwork they were working on.

Besides that, Alice had a habit of getting into bed as if she were mad at it. Ben had often told her that she got into bed like a 70 pound keg of nails.

His bedmate there sure didn't get into bed that way. It was a matter of kind of gently sliding into bed.

As Ben laid there, about to question Alice why she decided to come to bed after all, the second surprise came along. That surprise was in the form of a warm and gentle puff of breath on the back of his neck.

Now, Ben had been married long enough to know that Alice gently easing into bed, and giving him a provocative puff on his neck was totally out of character for her.

He turned to face her, and found a..........nothing, nothing at all. He had the bed all to himself, no wife, and no warm breath on the back of his neck.

Ben marveled at how he could be dreaming such a thing, not two minutes after laying down. He decided that he was even more tired than he thought, and had gotten to sleep as soon as he got that pillow squared away.

Ben went on to sleep with no further ado.

And, the project of fixing that house up continued. Ben was convinced that it was a never-ending job, and they'd be staining woodwork and hanging wallpaper when they were old and grey. But, he never did come up with a rebuttal to "It'll all work out alright."

It was about two weeks later, and Ben went to bed early again. He wasn't dead tired this time like the last time he had crawled in the sack alone, but just thought he'd get to bed early, and get up early.

The same routine...the laying on his side and the punching around on the pillow until it felt just right.

This time Ben hadn't yet even closed his eyes, and again there was that gentle sliding into bed next to him, followed by a provocative warm breath on the back of his neck.

Wow, this was just like that dream he had a couple weeks earlier, except this time he was awake. Ben wondered why Alice had suddenly taken up behavior that was so out of character for her.

"What's with your sliding into bed that way, Honey? What happened to your hitting the sack like you're mad at it?"

No answer.

"Honey, what's with your sneaking into bed that way?"

Again, no answer.

Twice he had talked to her, and she hadn't answered either time, so he turned so he could see her.............No Alice.........no anybody.

This time Ben knew he had something on his hands other than simply dreaming. Something was going on that needed explanation.

Ben laid there a moment, studying the pillow next to him when the thought struck him that this might be the work of a ghost. Alice was alive and well, he could hear her rattling the dishes

out in the kitchen as she cleaned up after their supper. It couldn't be Alice's ghost 'cause she wouldn't have one.

It was at that moment that he put two and two together and came up with the theory that his bedmate, temporary as she was, was the ghost of one of those fallen doves who had inhabited the house almost a hundred years earlier.

Now, good lookin' honeys softly sliding into bed with a fellow and puffing warm breath on his neck is something of a cause for celebration, even if she is a ghost.

Ben contemplated the situation as he laid there, about as wide awake as one person could be. He came to the conclusion that this house was a good idea, even if it was a lot of work and expense.

Sometimes there are intangible rewards in taking on a project, don't you know.

So, it was off to sleep for Ben, thinking of this good looking raven-haired beauty that had crawled into bed with him. Okay, so he made up the raven-haired part, but sometimes you have to improvise, you know.

Ben developed a new concern. He was concerned about the possibility that his experience that resulted from him going to bed early was not going to be repeated. He need not have feared that. From that point on, that happened a number of times.

Ben didn't bother Alice with all that. She had a lot on her mind, and he didn't want to unduly concern her. Ben was very considerate that way.

But, he chose to tell his buddies about his ghostly visitor. Actually, it was more of a case of bragging to his buddies about that.

Alice noticed that her husband had fewer bouts of wishing they hadn't gotten started on the B&B project. She was glad he was finally coming to see that things will all work out alright.

You know how things are. A buddy will tell his wife things, then his wife will talk to Alice and next thing you know, Alice knows all about the warm-breathed Honey.

It took some tall talking on Ben's part of explaining all that. He put it in the context of a dream, and how he only dreamed all that stuff, and he was really getting tired of having that same old tired dream every once in a while.

Ben took the precaution of holding his hand behind his back and crossing his fingers. He recalled that was a sure fire way of making it perfectly OK to cancel out the moral problem of telling a lie. He remembered that from his childhood. Everybody knew it was OK to lie if you crossed your fingers while doing so.

Surprisingly enough, Alice bought that. Perhaps she had been sniffing too many varnish fumes and didn't realize that Ben was lying through his teeth. They weren't dreams at all, much less dreams that Ben had tired of.

So, Alice put all that behind her. Besides that, you can't blame a fellow for having bad dreams, even if they are dreams about a ghost of a red-headed Honey. Ben had no idea where the "red headed" part came from, but figured that one of his buddies got the story wrong.

In spite of Alice's steadfast nature, the problems of redoing a large old Victorian house started to wear thin for her. So, when they discovered a leak in the roof that would require some expensive repair work, she wondered if they ought to give it up.

"You know, Ben, maybe what we ought to do is sell this place. You've been saying that for a long time now, and I think that maybe you're right."

Oops, this was a development that Ben wasn't ready for, much less come up with an argument against. He knew it was going to take some fancy footwork on his part to jump over to the other side of this "leave" or "not leave" issue.

"Yeah, well, we need to think about that, of course."

It was the best response Ben could come up with since he didn't have time there at the kitchen table to do the fancy footwork he needed to in order to switch sides on that issue.

"After all, Ben, when folks are paying a good price to stay in our B&B, they sure aren't going to appreciate what feels like a little honey crawling in bed with them and puffing warm breath on the back of their necks."

"Oh, no, of course not," Ben replied, hoping that he sounded half way sincere.

Having what seemed like Ben's agreement, Alice went on about how guys sure wouldn't want that inconvenience after a day's driving behind them, and another day's driving ahead of them.

Ben couldn't help but to think to himself..."What an inconvenience! What an inconvenience!"

This story took an unexpected turn as Ben was telling it to me.

"So, did Alice ever catch on to you?"

I had learned earlier from Ben that Alice had passed away shortly after the two of them finished up their B&B project. So, I wondered if she had learned about their ghost before she died.

"No," Ben said, "She never learned the truth, but there is sort of a sequel to this whole story."

"What's that?" I asked.

"Well, it wasn't long after Alice left us that those visits took on a new twist. The new twist was that if I'd go to be early, on occasion, I'd feel someone get into bed beside me, but after I lost Alice, it wasn't a matter of sliding into bed. It was still a ghost 'cause she'd be gone when I turned over."

"How, then, was it different?" I asked.

"It was different because after I lost Alice, my bed partner would get into bed like a 70 pound keg of nails........just like she was mad at the bed."

My Own Ghost Hunting Notes

My Own Ghost Hunting Notes

My Own Ghost Hunting Notes

My Own Ghost Hunting Notes

My Own Ghost Hunting Notes

My Own Ghost Hunting Notes

My Own Ghost Hunting Notes

My Own Ghost Hunting Notes

GHOSTS OF INTERSTATE 90 Chicago to Boston by D. Latham
GHOSTS of the Whitewater Valley by Chuck Grimes
GHOSTS of Interstate 74   by B. Carlson
GHOSTS of the Ohio Lakeshore Counties by Karen Waltemire
GHOSTS of Interstate 65   by Joanna Foreman
GHOSTS of Interstate 25 by Bruce Carlson
GHOSTS of the Smoky Mountains by Larry Hillhouse
GHOSTS of the Illinois Canal System by David Youngquist
GHOSTS of the Niagara River by Bruce Carlson
Ghosts of Little Bavaria   by Kishe Wallace

Shown above (at 85% of actual size) are the spines of other Quixote Press books of ghost stories. These are available at the retailer from whom this book was procured, or from our office at 1-800-571-2665 cost is $9.95 + $3.50 S/H.

- **GHOSTS of Lookout Mountain** by Larry Hillhouse
- *GHOSTS of Interstate 77* by Bruce Carlson
- **GHOSTS of Interstate 94** by B. Carlson
- **GHOSTS of MICHIGAN'S U. P.** by Chris Shanley-Dillman
- GHOSTS of the FOX RIVER VALLEY by D. Latham
- GHOSTS ALONG I-35 by B. Carlson
- **Ghostly Tales of Lake Huron** by Roger H. Meyer
- Ghost Stories by Kids, for Kids by some really great fifth graders
- Ghosts of Door County Wisconsin by Geri Rider
- *Ghosts of the Ozarks* B Carlson
- **Ghosts of US - 63** by Bruce Carlson
- *Ghostly Tales of Lake Erie* by Jo Lela Pope Kimber

Ghosts of Interstate 75	by Bruce Carlson
Ghosts of Lake Michigan	by Ophelia Julien
Ghosts of I-10	by C. J. Mouser
GHOSTS OF INTERSTATE 55	by Bruce Carlson
Ghosts of US - 13, Wisconsin Dells to Superior	by Bruce Carlson
Ghosts of I-80	David youngquist
Ghosts of Interstate 95	by Bruce Carlson
Ghosts of US 550	by Richard DeVore
Ghosts of Erie Canal	by Tony Gerst
Ghosts of the Ohio River	by Bruce Carlson
Ghosts of Warren County	by Various Writers
Ghosts of I-71 Louisville, KY to Cleveland, OH	by Bruce Carlson

GHOSTS OF DALLAS COUNTY	by Lori Pielak
Ghosts of US - 66 from Chicgo to Oklahoma	By McCarty & Wilson
Ghosts of the Appalachian Trail	by Dr. Tirstan Perry
Ghosts of I-70	by B. Carlson
Ghosts of the Thousand Islands	by Larry Hillhouse
Ghosts of US - 23 in Michigan	by B. Carlson
Ghosts of Lake Superior	by Enid Cleaves
GHOSTS OF THE IOWA GREAT LAKES	by Bruce Carlson
Ghosts of the Amana Colonies	by Lori Erickson
Ghosts of Lee County, Iowa	by Bruce Carlson
The Best of the Mississippi River Ghosts	by Bruce Carlson
Ghosts of Polk County Iowa	by Tom Welch

Ghosts of Ohio's Lake Erie shores & Islands Vacationland by B. Carlson
Ghosts of Des Moines County   by Bruce Carlson
Ghosts of the Wabash River   By Bruce Carlson
Ghosts of Michigan's US 127   by Bruce Carlson
GHOSTS OF I-79   *BY BRUCE CARLSON*
Ghosts of US-66 from Ft. Smith to Flagstaff   by Connie Wilson
Ghosts of US 6 in Pennsylvania   by Bruce Carlson
Ghosts of the Lower Missouri   by Marcia Schwartz
Ghosts of the Tennessee River in Tennessee   by Bruce Carlson
Ghosts of the Tennessee River in Alabama
Ghosts of Michigan's US 12 by R. Rademacher & B. Carlson
Ghosts of the Upper Savannah River from Augusta to Lake Hartwell   by Bruce Carlson
Mysteries of the Lake of the Ozarks   Hean & Sugar Hardin

To Order Copies

Please send me _____ copies of ***Ghosts of The Lincoln Highway In Ohio*** at $9.95 each plus $3.50 for the first one and $1.50 for each additional copy for S/H. (Make checks payable to **QUIXOTE PRESS**.)

Name _____

Street _____

City _____ State _____ Zip _____

QUIXOTE PRESS
3544 Blakslee Street
Wever, IA 52658
1-800-571-2665

To Order Copies

Please send me _____ copies of ***Ghosts of The Lincoln Highway In Ohio*** at $9.95 each plus $3.50 for the first one and $1.50 for each additional copy for S/H. (Make checks payable to **QUIXOTE PRESS**.)

Name _____

Street _____

City _____ State _____ Zip _____

QUIXOTE PRESS
3544 Blakslee Street
Wever, IA 52658
1-800-571-2665